Have fun counting and singing toget[h]
Watch the adorable song that
book and download free cour

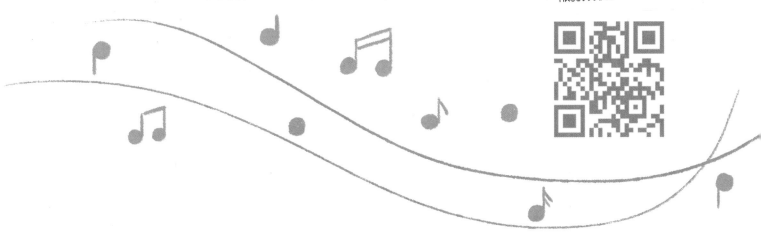

To my lovely sister.

Thank you for being with me
on every adventure,
no matter where the wind blows me.
My world is a better place
because of you.

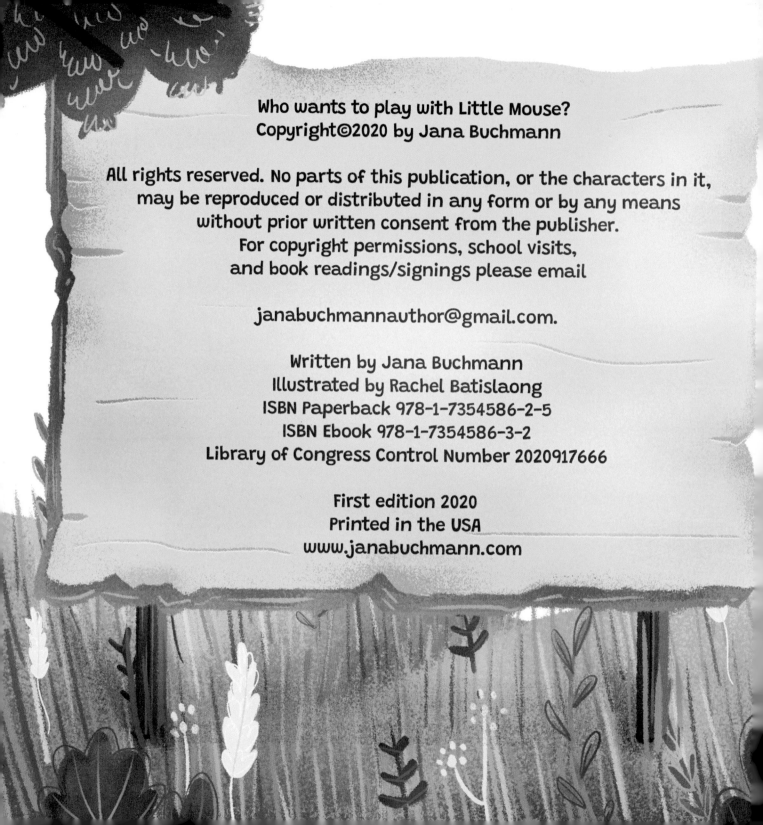

Written by Jana Buchmann
Illustrated by Rachel Batislaong
ISBN Paperback 978-1-7354586-2-5
ISBN Ebook 978-1-7354586-3-2
Library of Congress Control Number 2020917666

First edition 2020
Printed in the USA
www.janabuchmann.com

Who Wants to Play With LITTLE MOUSE?

Written by Jana Buchmann

Illustrated by Rachel Batislaong

Behind the trees lived Little Mouse.
His house was nice and cozy.
But he felt lonely one hot day,
with just one plant named Rosie.

The sun was warm and shining bright
from high up in the sky.
So Little Mouse set out to see
his friends, who lived nearby.

One busy ant ran through the grass
and didn't want to stop.
She had some news to bring along
and rushed up to the top.

2

Two birds flew by
and sang a song.
Lil' Mouse looked up
and smiled.
But then the birds
went with the wind,
away into the wild.

3

Three spiders spun their silky webs
to catch some beams of sun.
They didn't hear poor Little Mouse
who asked to have some fun.

Four crickets made a funny sound
atop the great gray stone.
The concert didn't seem to end,
and Mouse left all alone.

Five frogs jumped high
and had much fun.
They splashed into the pond.
"Oh, let me join!"
called Little Mouse.
The frogs did not respond.

Six snails with houses
on their backs
crept in a slimy row.
They didn't notice Little Mouse
and slid away real slow.

Seven bees came flying by
and looked around for food.
They buzzed above
his head without
a look at him. How rude!

Eight worms were digging
in the dirt
to find a nice cool place.
They didn't see
sweet Little Mouse
and vanished with no trace.

Nine ducks went swimming
in the pond
while quacking in the sun.
They couldn't hear Mouse
asking them
if he could join the fun.

Ten bugs marched slowly in a line
and made a stop to play.
Oh no! A sneeze from Little Mouse
blew all the bugs away!

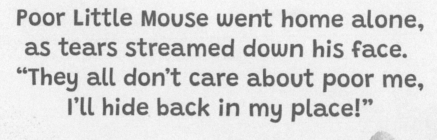

Poor Little Mouse went home alone,
as tears streamed down his face.
"They all don't care about poor me,
I'll hide back in my place!"

Next day, he heard a funny noise,
some giggles and a shout.

"Let's all count back
from ten to one!"

"My friends!"

Lil' Mouse cried out.

"TEN!" said the bugs.

"NINE!" quacked the ducks.

"EIGHT!" cried the worms.

"SEVEN!" buzzed the bees.

"SIX!" called the snails.

"FIVE!" quaked the frogs

"FOUR!" chirped the crickets.

"THREE!" whooped the spiders.

"TWO!" sang the birds.

"ONE!" yelled the ant.

His friends said,

"We are sorry, Mouse!"

and then they squeezed him tight.

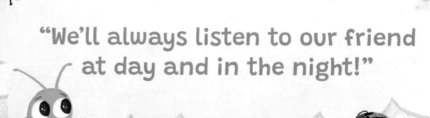
"We'll always listen to our friend
at day and in the night!"

So, Little Mouse danced happily
and looked up to the sun.
He knew his friends would not forget
their friendship and their fun!

Jana Buchmann is a children's book author and mom of three girls with a love of storytelling. She enjoys combining unique ideas with magic and imagination to create memorable stories that bring tons of fun and smiles to every child who reads them.

When not writing, Jana enjoys reading, traveling, being creative, and spending time with her three wonderful daughters. She also volunteers for an organization that reads and streams children's books for kids in a hospital.

For more information visit:
janabuchmann.com

Visit www.janabuchmann.com for free activity booklets and creative ideas to spark your child's imagination.

f **janabuchmannauthor**

◎ **janabuchmann_author**

More books from the author:

More coming soon! To be the first in the know, subscribe to my newsletter here: www.janabuchmann.com.

Rachel "Cheng" Batislaong is an artist/illustrator from the Philippines. She studied Fine Arts and has worked with several advertising agencies. She's now living her dream of becoming a children's book illustrator and has loved it ever since.

She has illustrated books for clients in the Philippines, USA, Qatar, UK and Canada.

She likes it when she's called "Cheng".

For inquiries, feel free to email her at

chengbatislaong@gmail.com

More of Cheng's artworks here:

 chengpb_art

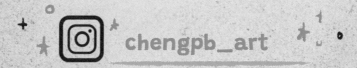 Cheng Batislaong

 Cheng Batislaong

Made in the USA
Las Vegas, NV
15 January 2021